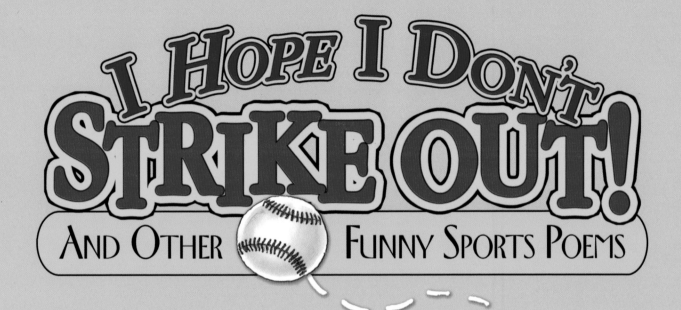

I Hope I Don't Strike Out!

And Other Funny Sports Poems

Created By
Bruce Lansky
"King of Giggle Poetry"

Meadowbrook Press
Distributed by Simon & Schuster
New York

Library of Congress Cataloging-in-Publication Data

I hope I don't strike out! and other funny sports poems / edited by Bruce Lansky ; illustrated by Stephen Carpenter.
   p. cm.
  Summary: "A collection of humorous poems about kids and sports"–Provided by publisher.
  ISBN-10: 0-88166-535-5, ISBN-13: 978-0-88166-535-2 (Meadowbrook Press);
ISBN 10: 1-41695-198-9, ISBN 13: 978-1-4169-5198-8 (Simon & Schuster)
  1. Sports–Juvenile poetry. 2. Children's poetry, American. 3. Humorous poetry, American.
I. Lansky, Bruce. II. Carpenter, Stephen, ill.
  PS595.S78I 2008
  811'.54080355–dc22

2007023798

Coordinating Editor and Copyeditor: Angela Wiechmann
Editorial Assistant and Proofreader: Alicia Ester
Production Manager: Paul Woods
Graphic Design Manager: Tamara Peterson
Illustrations and Cover Art: © Stephen Carpenter

© 2008 by Meadowbrook Creations

Published by Meadowbrook Press, 6110 Blue Circle Drive, Suite 237, Minnetonka, Minnesota 55343

www.meadowbrookpress.com

BOOK TRADE DISTRIBUTION by Simon and Schuster, a division of Simon and Schuster, Inc., 1230 Avenue of the Americas, New York, New York 10020

17 16 15 14 13 12   10 9 8 7 6 5 4 3 2

Printed in Mexico

Credits

"Jimmy Cho's Karate School" © 2008 by Steve Charney; "The School Olympics" © 2008 by Pat Dodds; "Great Day on the Golf Course," "I Hope I Don't Strike Out!" "Three Strikes and You're Out," and "Victory Cheer" © 2008 by Bruce Lansky; "Hockey Team" © 2008 by Neal Levin; "They Say That Sports Are Good for You" © 2008 by Judith Natelli McLaughlin; "How I Became a Black Belt" © 2008 by Jeff Mondak; "Take Me Out of the Ball Game" © 2006 by Jeff Nathan, previously published in *Oh My Darling, Porcupine*; "Ski Trip" © 2008 by Jeff Nathan; "Our Teacher's a Football Fanatic" © 2007 by Kenn Nesbitt, previously published in *Revenge of the Lunch Ladies*; "Deep-Sea Squeeze" and "We're Going Skiing" © 2008 by Eric Ode; "As I Was Sprinting Home Today" and "The Score Is Tied, My Knees Are Weak" © 2008 by Paul Orshoski; "Peewee Soccer" © 2007 by Robert Pottle, previously published in *I'm Allergic to School!*; "The Race" © 2008 by Robert Pottle; "The Fastest Kid in School" © 2008 by Darren Sardelli; "The Duke of Dodge Ball" © 2008 by Ted Scheu; "Excuse Cheer" © 2004 by Tim Tocher, previously published in *Rolling in the Aisles*; and "Relay Race" © 2008 by Stan Lee Werlin.

Acknowledgments

Many thanks to the following teachers and their students who tested poems for this anthology: Kathy Austrian, Lakeway Elementary, Austin, TX; Michael Bowman, Robertsville School, Morganville, NJ; Dawn Carlson, East Elementary, New Richmond, WI; Diane Clapp, Lincoln Elementary, Fairbault, MN; Niki Danou, Groveland Elementary, Minnetonka, MN; Jeremy Engebretson, Groveland Elementary, Minnetonka, MN; Sandy Kane, Lincoln Elementary, Fairbault, MN; Kathy Kenney-Marshall, McCarthy Elementary, Framingham, MA; Carolyn Larsen, Rum River Elementary, Andover, MN; Carol Larson, Rum River Elementary, Andover, MN; Maren Morgan-Thomson, District-Topton Elementary, Topton, PA; Jenny Myer, East Elementary, New Richmond, WI; Hope Nadeau, East Elementary, New Richmond, WI; Ruth Refsnider, East Elementary, New Richmond, WI; Beverly Semanko, Rum River Elementary, Andover, MN; Maria Smith, Deer Creek Elementary, Crowley, TX; Suzanne Storbeck, Holy Name School, Wayzata, MN; Lisa Thorne, Butler Elementary, Bulter, OH; Carleen Tjader, East Elementary, New Richmond, WI; Margaret Weiss, East Elementary, New Richmond, WI; and Julie White, Media Specialist, East Elementary, New Richmond, WI

Contents

I Hope I Don't Strike Out!

I was substituted in the game in inning number nine.
I'd been sitting on the bench because the game was on the line.
Our first baseman had the runs and so his cleanup spot was mine.
I hope I don't strike out!

Well, the bases all were loaded, and the pressure sure was high.
When the going's tough, the tough get going—I'm not that kind of guy.
But if I strike out, we'll lose the game, then I'll break down and cry.
I hope I don't strike out!

The pitcher took one look at me and knew I was no threat.
He could see my hands were shaking and my uniform was wet.
He bragged, "My fastball's smokin'. I will strike you out, no sweat."
I hope I don't strike out!

Well, the first pitch was a bullet, and the umpire yelled, "Strike one!"
I couldn't swing the bat because it seemed to weigh a ton.
If the pitcher threw two more like that, we'd lose by just a run.
I hope I don't strike out!

The second pitch came at me, and I thought I saw it dance.
The knuckler dipsy-doodled, then it breezed right by my pants.
The umpire yelled "Strike two!" before I woke out of a trance.
I hope I don't strike out!

Then from the seats along third base, I heard a voice I knew.
My father waved and yelled again, "Don't worry—don't be blue.
Just keep your eyes upon the ball, and you might hit a few.
I hope you don't strike out."

Well, my back was to the pitcher as he let the third pitch fly.
I was waving to my dad and thinking, "What a thoughtful guy."
My bat was on my shoulder—that's the only reason why...
I didn't swing and miss.

Well, the ball bounced off my bat and slowly dribbled toward first base.
The catcher tore his mask off, and I watched him giving chase.
My coach yelled, "Run!" I dropped my bat, and I was in a race.
That's how I made a hit!

Our fans were wildly cheering as the opposition frowned.
Their tears were flowing as they stood with eyes upon the ground.
They didn't see two runners score who didn't make a sound.
That's how we won the game!

Bruce Lansky

Peewee Soccer

Christopher is counting clouds.
Hannah braids her hair.
Peter's playing peekaboo.
Greg growls like a bear.

Kevin kicks with all his might,
and though the ball stays put,
his sneaker sails across the field
to land near Roger's foot.

Roger starts to kick the shoe.
Soon poor Kevin's crying.
Katie gives the ball a kick
and sends that ball a-flying.

Billy Brown is looking down.
He sees a four-leaf clover.
Billy wants to pick the plant,
and that's why he bends over.

We see the ball bounce off his bum
and then sail toward the goal.
The goalie gets confused.
We watch him stop then drop and roll.

The other team lets out a cheer
and our team starts to scream
as Billy's bottom scores a goal
for the other team.

Robert Pottle

5

Victory Cheer

V-I-C-T-O-R-Y!
When we win this game, you'll cry.
You will run home to your mamas,
dress for bed in pink pajamas.

You can pout and hide your head
under covers in your bed.
Even if you lock the door,
that won't change the final score.

That is why we love this cheer
and shout it loud so you can hear.
We will win 'cause we know how.
You might as well stop playing now!

Bruce Lansky

6

Excuse Cheer

Our center's nose was runny. Our forwards had the flu.
The guards were feeling funny. That's why we lost to you.
Your team is overrated. We really didn't try.
Our coach was constipated. I'm telling you no lie.
Now go and take a shower and hop back on your bus.
You know we'll beat you next time, so you'd best watch out for us!

Tim Tocher

Great Day on the Golf Course

(sing to the tune of "My Bonnie")

I had a great time on the golf course.
My dad took me out for the day.
He got me to go when he promised
I'd drive the golf cart all the way.

Chorus

    Golfing, golfing,
    I had a great day on the
    course with Dad.
    Golfing, golfing,
    I had a great day on the course.

My dad hit a drive off the tee box
so far that it sailed out of view.
It landed too close to some golfers.
They swore they were going to sue.

Chorus

I drove down a hill on the fairway.
I steered the golf cart off a bump.
My dad thought his heart had stopped beating.
His head got a big, nasty lump.

Chorus

My dad hit a ball in the bunker.
He took seven shots to get out.
I counted out loud every time that he missed.
And that's when he started to shout.

Chorus

My dad hit three balls in the water.
I rolled up my pants for a swim.
I found all three balls underwater
and sold all three balls back to him.

Chorus

While putting, my father bent over.
He lined up the putt without fear.
But just as he started his backswing,
I snapped his golf towel at his rear.

Chorus

I had a great time at the golf course.
I told my dad, "Gee, thanks a lot."
My mom was surprised when I told her,
"I didn't take one single shot."

Bruce Lansky

Jimmy Cho's Karate School

(sing to the tune of "Oh, Christmas Tree")

We use our forehead as a rule
in Jimmy Cho's Karate School
to break a board or crush a stool
in Jimmy Cho's Karate School.
We have to wear these funny clothes.
You laugh, but that's just how it goes.
Our clothes look dumb, but we are cool
in Jimmy Cho's Karate School.

You better not dare ridicule
the kids at Cho's Karate School,
or you'll be fighting in a duel
at Jimmy Cho's Karate School.
With fifty pairs of smelly feet,
our lockers don't smell very sweet.
We kick and shout and sometimes drool
in Jimmy Cho's Karate School.

Steve Charney

How I Became a Black Belt

A week ago Sunday with weather so warm,
karate class met in the park.
We practiced our kicks, then we studied our form
and chopped at the sycamore bark.

I sat and I rested beneath that great tree
while Christopher worked on his stance.
My mind was so focused that I didn't see
the ants marching straight up my pants.

The ants in my britches were biting me there.
The bite marks were starting to swell.
I itched, so I kicked and I clawed at the air,
then spun as I let out a yell.

I twirled and I jumped with such dizzying speed
while trying to scratch at the bites.
The teachers looked on and then quickly agreed
my skills had reached masterful heights.

For twenty-three minutes I pranced without pause.
I shrieked at each itchy red welt.
I finished at last to the master's applause.
He bowed and he gave me his belt.

Jeff Mondak

As I Was Sprinting Home Today

As I was sprinting home today,
a gang of thugs appeared.
They roughed me up. They scratched my face.
And for my life I feared.

They tackled me and piled on.
They left me feeling dazed.
They pulled my hair. They ripped my clothes.
I tell you, they were crazed.

But as the rowdy group withdrew,
I knew it was in fun.
My baseball team had won its game—
I scored the winning run.

Paul Orshoski

They Say That Sports Are Good for You

When jogging just the other day,
I ran into a tree.

While hiking with my friends from school,
I tripped and skinned my knee.

In tennis, I returned a serve
by using my right eye.

In basketball, I blocked a shot,
but crashed on the deny.

I broke my leg while skiing.
Playing golf, I wrenched my neck.

I tried my hand at sailing,
but I fell right off the deck.

They say that sports are good for you—
a workout clears your head.

I think it's better for my health
if I just watch instead.

Judith Natelli McLaughlin

13

We're Going Skiing

My friend Martha called this morning
with this happy, hurried warning:
"I asked Mom, and she's agreeing.
Grab your stuff! We're going skiing!"

Nothing could have sounded better.
In a flash, I found my sweater,
then my gloves—a matching pair.
Next, my winter underwear.

Grabbed a parka, warm and fat.
Found my scarf and woolen hat.
Soon I heard a car arriving.
Martha's mother, she was driving.

Martha gave a happy shout.
All my buddies tumbled out,
cheering with a loud commotion,
throwing towels and suntan lotion.

What an unexpected sight!
Something simply wasn't right.
I was in my scarf and boots.
They were in their swimming suits.

Martha stopped and scratched her head.
"Sorry if we stare," she said.
"Maybe we're not used to seeing
clothes like those for water-skiing."

Eric Ode

14

The Duke of Dodge Ball

I'm called the "Duke of Dodge Ball,"
the greatest in the game.
Against the best, I never rest
at putting kids to shame.

I wear my crown with confidence,
and much to their dismay,
opposing teams have scary dreams
the night before we play.

It's not that I am lightning quick
or have a rocket throw.
My arms are limp spaghetti, and
my feet are turtle slow.

Instead, I use a strategy
of wiliness and wit:
I hide behind the biggest boys
until they all get hit.

When they go out, I follow them.
I sit and wait, and then,
when all the balls are on our side,
I shout, "Hey, I'm still in!"

So cheer the "Duke of Dodge Ball,"
and celebrate my reign.
You can't deny I'm super sly;
I really use my brain!

Ted Scheu

The School Olympics

We had the School Olympics
in my classroom yesterday.
I won six gold medals,
I am very proud to say.

To start the day, I came in first
in running down the hall.
I knocked a few kids over,
and I didn't even fall.

I hurdled over Teacher's desk
and landed in his chair.
A lot of stuff fell on the floor.
I hope he didn't care.

I shot a bunch of rubber bands
and hit the target—*splat!*
The boy who sits in front of me
yelled, "Ouch! Hey, what was that?"

I threw a great big water bottle
neatly in the trash.
It flew at least a dozen yards
and never made a splash.

I kicked my backpack in the air.
I kicked it really high.
It landed way up on the roof,
and Teacher just said, "Why?"

At recess time I took a dive
into a pool of mud.
I went to class a little wet.
My friends said, "Where's the flood?"

And now the games are over.
No more medals can I win.
My teacher says I'll have to wait
four years to play again.

                    Pat Dodds

Our Teacher's a Football Fanatic

Our teacher's a football fanatic.
It's all that he has on his mind.
He listens to games on his headphones
and frets when his team is behind.

He jumps up and down when they're winning.
He screams when they fumble a pass.
We know we're supposed to be reading,
but watching him's simply a gas.

Our principal walked in on Friday,
and he was too angry to speak.
Our substitute started on Monday.
Our teacher's been
    benched for a week.

Kenn Nesbitt

Hockey Team

I want to join the hockey team.
I think it would be cool.
They're always leaving early
in the afternoon from school.

They say they have to practice
and they need an early start.
They get to miss geography
and algebra and art.

They say they have a game tonight
and have to go get dressed.
They get to skip the rest of class
and get to miss the test.

I want to join the hockey team.
Who cares if I'm a rookie?
They really don't play hockey much.
They mainly just play hooky.

Neal Levin

19

The Score Is Tied, My Knees Are Weak

The score is tied, my knees are weak,
and time is running out.
The referee needs glasses,
and our winning streak's in doubt.

I've bitten off my fingernails.
My stomach is in knots.
I think I am about to faint,
and now I'm seeing spots.

My heart is racing swiftly.
My legs are getting tight.
My palms are moist and clammy.
My knuckles just turned white.

I'm sweating so profusely,
I'm giving off a stench.
And I'm not even in the game—
I'm sitting on the bench.

Paul Orshoski

Take Me Out of the Ball Game
(sing to the tune of "Take Me Out to the Ball Game")

Take me out of the ball game.
Take me off of the mound.
Get me out quickly—oh, please don't wait.
I throw hard, but I can't reach home plate.
I just walked another four runs in.
If we don't win, I'm to blame.
And it's one, two, three strikes, I'm out
when I play this game.

Take me out of the ball game.
Take me out right away.
Why did you put me at second base?
Every hit makes me cover my face.
I just broke the record for errors.
If we don't win, I'm to blame.
And it's one, two, three strikes, I'm out
when I play this game.

Take me out of the ball game.
Take me out of right field.
Put someone in who won't trip and fall—
anyone who can catch a fly ball.
Now I just missed my fourteenth grounder.
If we don't win, I'm to blame.
And it's one, two, three strikes, I'm out
when I play this game.

Take me out of the ball game.
It's my turn up at bat.
I swing and miss, but it's no surprise.
I'm too frightened to open my eyes.
And I heard strike three whizzing past me.
If we don't win, I'm to blame.
For it's one, two, three strikes, I'm out
when I play this game.

Jeff Nathan

Relay Race

The annual neighborhood relay and race
began with a bang and a blistering pace.
The starter called "Go!" as he fired his gun,
but it didn't work out well for Team Number One!

Benjamin Blunderbean grabbed the baton,
slipped at the starting line, slid on the lawn,
fell on his face on the way up the street,
tangled his arms in his legs and his feet.
Benjamin bumbled and bounced off a tree,
ruined his sneakers and injured his knee,
plopped in a puddle and stepped on a bee,
then he passed the baton on to Jenny.

Jennifer jumped in a jungle of weed,
lost her new socks while she gathered up speed,
ran through some rosebushes, scraped both her legs,
stopped at a traffic light, ate scrambled eggs.
Jennifer dawdled through hill and through dale.
All of her friends cried, "You're slow as a snail!"
Finally found her way back to the trail,
and she passed the baton on to Bethany.

Bethany Brett had no sense of direction,
quickly got lost, and ran on in dejection,
stopped for a movie and stayed for an hour,
ran to Chicago and climbed up a tower.
Finally Bethany found her way back,
saw all her friends waiting 'round at the track.
"Hurry!" they called to her. "Get out the slack!"
And she passed the baton on to Sara.

Sara the Streak, she was faster than fast.
That's why they saved her to always go last.
Running so swiftly, she rose like a rocket,
sailed through the sky, and came down in Woonsocket,
passed through New Jersey, Virginia, and 'Bama,
hitchhiked a ride on a motorized llama.
Long after sundown she raced even faster,
but out in the desert she had a disaster.

All of her friends at the finishing line
waited for Sara and looked for a sign.
She came back at midnight stuck tight to a cactus—
good thing today it was only a practice!
Stan Lee Werlin

Ski Trip

We all went on a ski trip—
my dad and me and Paul.
We packed our warmest clothing.
It's freezing, after all.

And early in the morning,
we headed for the lift.
But Paul was acting funny.
He didn't look too swift.

We hit the Double Diamonds.
I waited at the top.
My dad pulled up beside me,
but Paul just couldn't stop.

When turning, we do pole plants—
it helps us turn at will.
But Paul, he did a face plant
and tumbled down the hill.

His skis went flying skyward,
then down he slid headfirst.
With snow packed in his jacket,
he looked like he might burst.

So, in between our laughing,
we helped collect his junk.
We asked him what had caused him
to ski like such a punk.

He told us of the blunder
that he had made last night:
He'd packed his sister's long johns,
and they were way too tight.

We haven't stopped our laughter
about this whole affair.
We tease Paul 'cause he skied in
his sister's underwear.

Jeff Nathan

25

The Fastest Kid in School

I am the fastest kid in school.
I have the fastest feet.
There's no one who can match my speed.
I simply can't be beat.
There's nothing you can say or do
to beat me in this race.
We may be racing side by side,
but I will win first place.

Before I leave you in the dust,
there's something you should know:
I'll beat you skating on the ice
and running through the snow.
I'll beat you on a ten-speed bike.
I'll beat you in the pool.
I'll beat you sprinting up the stairs
and down the halls in school.

Prepare to feel embarrassed
when I beat you on this track.
I'll beat you running backward
with my hands behind my back.
You may have run ahead of me,
but now you're going down!
I plan to show these people
I'm the fastest kid in town!

I'm gonna—*ouch*! I'm cramping up!
My ankles are in pain!
My belly hurts! My back is out!
My shoes are filled with rain!
I'll win on any other day.
Just pick the time and place.
I know you think you beat me,
but I let you win the race!

Darren Sardelli

The Race

We hear the bell, and we begin.
All will race. One will win.

Murphy's running first with pride—
doesn't know his shoe's untied.

When he crashes in the hall,
down fall Tasha, Keith, and Paul.

I steer around the wreck with skill.
I'm gonna win. I can. I will!

I'm moving fast with super speed.
Hey, I'm first! I'm in the lead.

I round the corner. There's the bus.
Those behind are eating dust.

I'm on the bus. I'm first. I win!
Tomorrow we will race again.

PE's great, but not as cool
as when we get to leave the school.

Robert Pottle

Deep-Sea Squeeze

I'm wrapped from top to bottom
in an octopus embrace
with seven arms around my waist
and one across my face.

It all began this morning
with a scuba diving trip.
I found the creature wedged beneath
a sunken pirate ship.

So, carefully I dug him free.
He offered no objection,
but covered me in tentacles
with octopus affection.

It seems I've made a friend today,
but this I'd like to know:
How do you say in Octopus,
"You're welcome. Please let go."

Eric Ode